This book is awarded to

....

The Wildlife Winter Games

Written by Richard Turner
Illustrated by Ben Clifford

For creatures that play games in the cold,
there are medals of **bronze**, silver and gold.
In the 10 events of the winter games,
to have fun and compete are the aims.

Who do you think will take the prize?
Is it down to strength, speed, or size?
Take a look at the pages within.
Can you predict who might win?

The Wildlife Winter Games take place on snow and ice. How do you think the experts on snow and ice, the Arctic and Antarctic creatures, would fare if they used their unique skills to compete against each other?

In each of the ten events, three different creatures will compete against each other. Select who you think will win the **bronze**, silver and gold medals!

The Wildlife Winter Games begin with the athletes marching proudly into the stadium. The Wildlife Winter Games' symbol of a snowflake embraced by a feather, paw print, and scales represents all competitors, whether they are of the air, land, or water.

How many different creatures can you name?

ICE HOCKEY

This fast-paced team sport requires skill, speed, agility, and endurance. Which team will score the bronze, silver, and gold — the plucky penguins, the pugnacious polar bears, or the wily wolverines?

 PENGUINS – They waddle when they walk, but give them a hockey stick and skates and they're right at home on the ice. What they lack in size they make up for with speed and skill. Great teamwork is the strength of these social creatures.

 POLAR BEARS – They may look cuddly, but they are powerful and ferocious. Their huge paws are an advantage when defending the goal. However, they are not fast due to their size, and with their thick fur, they can overheat!

 WOLVERINES – They are short, stocky, tough, and tenacious. They are fierce competitors who never give up. Can these solitary creatures work together to win?

 PUFFIN – It has excellent flying skills and can dive into water to catch prey. It has adapted these acrobatic skills for the ice to produce spectacular routines. With wings that can flap up to 400 times a minute, will it fly away with the gold?

 RINGED SEAL – This seal may be the smallest to come out of the Arctic, but it is a flexible and graceful swimmer. Will its elite swimming skills help it to skate rings around the opposition?

FIGURE SKATING

Whose routine will catch the eye of the judges to win the gold — the perky puffin, the sassy seal, or the oceanic octopus?

 ANTARCTIC OCTOPUS – It lives at the bottom of the Southern Ocean and moves along using jet propulsion. This is an asset on the ice for a burst of speed to launch into spectacular jumps and spins. Are eight skates an advantage on the ice?

BOBSLED

Teams aim for the fastest time sliding down a winding icy track in a sled. Which team of four will slip and slide to glory — the sleek sea otters, the lively lemmings, or the sublime snow geese?

 SEA OTTERS – Under water, their nostrils and ears close over. This is an asset on the sled, as it reduces wind drag. They keep their waterproof coats in perfect condition, making them even more aerodynamic. Will they clean up the opposition?

 LEMMINGS – In their Arctic habitat, they make runways and tunnels under snow, so they are suited to racing along narrow tracks. Though small, they are fierce and can fight off larger animals. Will they run away with the gold?

 SNOW GOOSE – Its long neck, when arched forward with its small head and pointed bill, makes it aerodynamic. Its short legs allow it to get down low in the sled to further lessen wind drag. Will they fly down the track to take the gold?

 ARCTIC FOX – Its body is only 65 cm (25.6 in) long, and its bushy tail, called a brush, is 30 cm (11.8 in) long. Its large tail helps keep it warm in the wild and helps with balance, which is important in ski jumping. Will it be able to brush its opponents aside to win?

 SNOW PETREL – This bird flies around cliffs in the Antarctic at high speed, climbing, diving, and changing direction with a twist of its wings. Will its acrobatic skills help it ski away with the gold?

SKIING

In the freestyle aerials, who has what it takes to impress the judges with their take off from the ski jump, their acrobatic flips and twists in the air, and their landing — the audacious Arctic fox, the sizzling snow petrel, or the scintillating stoat?

 STOAT – Its slender, agile body allows it to travel swiftly on the snow in a zigzag pattern, moving in a series of leaps. Will its athletic skills help it flip, twist, and turn its way to glory?

SPEED SKATING

Speed skaters need a quick start, endurance, and agility. Who can speedily skate their way to victory — the agile Arctic hare, the muscular moose, or the masterly musk ox?

 ARCTIC HARE – It may be small, but it is extremely quick, reaching speeds of 64 km/h (39.8 mi/h) to evade predators. That's fast! It will be very hard to catch.

 MUSK OX – It is stocky with short legs but can still run at speeds up to 40 km/h (24.9 mi/h). Will its long thick coat help or hinder its chances of winning the gold?

 MOOSE – With its long legs, it is one of the fastest runners in its forest habitat, reaching speeds of 56 km/h (34.8 mi/h). Even though the moose is strong and powerful, do you think its huge antlers are an advantage or disadvantage when speed skating?

 ORCA – The orca or killer whale is actually a dolphin. It uses echolocation, bouncing sound waves off objects to receive information about distance and location. Will this unique skill steer it to the gold?

 SOUTHERN ELEPHANT SEAL – This large seal is an excellent swimmer and diver. Its flexible body is shaped like a torpedo, making it aerodynamic on the sled. Can it torpedo the opposition to win gold?

LUGE

Luge racers aim for the fastest time, speeding down a slippery ice track on a sled, relying on reflexes for steering. Who will record the fastest time — the slick seal, the overpowering orca, or the gigantic Greenland shark?

 GREENLAND SHARK – Though not a fast swimmer, its large size and weight helps its sled speed down the icy track. While its eyesight is poor, it has an amazing sense of smell. Will it follow the scent to the gold medal?

CURLING

Teams of four take turns sliding eight polished 'rocks' toward a target marked on an ice rink. Two team members sweep the ice with special brooms to control the path of the rock. Who will sweep to the gold — the wise walrus, the heady harp seal or the crafty colossal squid?

 WALRUS – The two tusks are actually teeth that can grow up to 1 m (3.3 ft) long. They also have air sacs in their throat, which enables them to sleep while swimming. Will they be caught napping and miss out on the gold?

 HARP SEAL – Their whiskers give them an excellent sense of touch. They also have powerful vision and a strong sense of smell. Will sensory powers help defeat the larger walrus and squid?

 COLOSSAL SQUID – They are the largest invertebrates in the world, with the largest eyes in the animal kingdom. Will this help them keep their eye on the target?

 NARWHAL – This unique whale is called the unicorn of the ocean due to its tusk, which is actually a long tooth. Will its weight help it reach the speed needed to perform dynamic flips and turns?

 ARCTIC TERN – This is an athletic flier, swooping and dipping down to the water to catch its prey. Will having wings be an advantage on the snowboard?

SNOWBOARD

A snowboard is used in the Half Pipe event to perform acrobatic tricks while going from one side of a semi-circular pipe to the other. Who can out-trick the opposition — the nifty narwhal, the ace Arctic tern, or the heroic hourglass dolphin?

 HOURGLASS DOLPHIN – It enjoys riding wave and can even change direction to catch waves made by boats, ships, and even whales! Will this nimble swimmer ride the snowboard to the gold medal?

SKI JUMPING

Jumps are scored on the distance travelled and style of the jump. Who can perform the longest and most stylish jumps — the astonishing albatross, the sprightly snowshoe hare, or the adventurous Arctic wolf?

 ALBATROSS – It has a wingspan of 3 m (9.8 ft), the largest of any bird, and can glide for hours without a flap of its wings! While amazing in the air, does it have the style to match?

 SNOWSHOE HARE – It is larger than a rabbit, with taller hind legs and longer ears. It has especially large, furry feet that help it move quickly atop snow. Will these features help it stylishly out-leap the opposition?

 ARCTIC WOLF – One of the toughest creatures on the planet, it lives in an extremely harsh habitat. For five months of the year, it lives in darkness. It can go months without eating and will travel hundreds of km's (mi's) to find food. Will this adaptable creature find a way to win?

 BALD EAGLE – This powerful bird combines amazing flying with excellent eyesight. It can spot prey from great distances before swooping to grasp it in its talons. Does it have the winning combination of endurance and accuracy?

 DALL SHEEP – It inhabits mountain ranges, so it is an excellent climber with great endurance. Its age can be determined by counting the rings on its unusual horns, as a new ring forms each year. Can it count on its skills to win the gold?

BIATHLON

The Biathlon's two events are cross-country skiing and target shooting. Who can best combine endurance for skiing and accuracy for target shooting — the brash bald eagle, crafty caribou, or dexterous Dall sheep?

 CARIBOU – Also called a reindeer, it has great endurance, travelling as many as 2,500 km (1,553.4 mi) in its yearly migration. An excellent climber, with strong legs that help it travel over deep snow, does it have the skills to target the gold?

The winter games fun is done.
Ten events have been played and won.
On the ice and over the snow,
creatures have put on a show
with their skills and natural flair,
over the ground and in the air.
Was it down to strength, speed, or size?
How did you decide who'd take the prize?

Starfish Bay® Children's Books
An imprint of Starfish Bay Publishing
www.starfishbaypublishing.com

THE WILDLIFE WINTER GAMES

Text copyright © Richard Turner, 2019
Illustrations copyright © Ben Clifford, 2019
ISBN 978-1-76036-075-7
First Published 2019
Printed in China by Toppan Leefung Printing Limited
20th Floor, 169 Electric Road, North Point, Hong Kong

Sincere thanks to Elyse Williams from Starfish Bay Children's Books for her creative efforts in preparing this edition for publication.

For Mandy,

Thank you for your kindness, consideration and sparks of inspiration. – R.T.

Richard Turner is a Performing Arts teacher in Australia, who supports children's creative voices through drama and dance. He has directed and choreographed musicals, working with students who can sing and dance way better than he can. Like most children, Richard has to be told to eat his peas, but never has to be told to eat his jellybeans or ice cream. He has been on a skateboard, a rollercoaster, an elephant and a camel. He has also been on a spaceship to the moon, but only in his dreams!

For my brothers Brett and Mathew

Ben Clifford was born and raised in Tasmania, Australia. He began illustrating after living in the snow with the badgers and brown hares in England. After returning home, Ben began drawing, painting, illustrating and writing books. When he's not drawing or writing stories, running through forests, climbing mountains or kayaking in rivers, he loves to snowboard and throw snowballs at his friends.